This is a Borzoi Book published by Alfred A. Knopf, a division of Random House, Inc.

Copyright © 1999, 2001 by Hachette Livre
All rights reserved under International and Pan-American Copyright
Conventions. Published in the United States of America by Alfred A. Knopf,
a division of Random House, Inc., New York, and simultaneously in Canada by
Random House of Canada Limited, Toronto. Distributed by Random House, Inc.,
New York. Originally published in France as Lisa prend l'avion by Hachette
Jeunesse in 1999. KNOPF, BORZOI BOOKS, and the colophon are registered
trademarks of Random House, Inc.
www.randomhouse.com/kids
Library of Congress Catalog Card Number: 00-131160
ISBN 0-375-81114-1
First Borzoi Books edition: March 2001
Printed in France   10 9 8 7 6 5 4 3 2 1

Lisa's Airplane Trip

ANNE GUTMAN · GEORG HALLENSLEBEN

Alfred A. Knopf · New York

I'm Lisa.

Guess where I was last week?

In a **BIG** plane over the ocean.

I was flying by myself for the very first time.

My seat was next to a blue lady.
"Don't be afraid," she said, "and please
try not to move around so much."

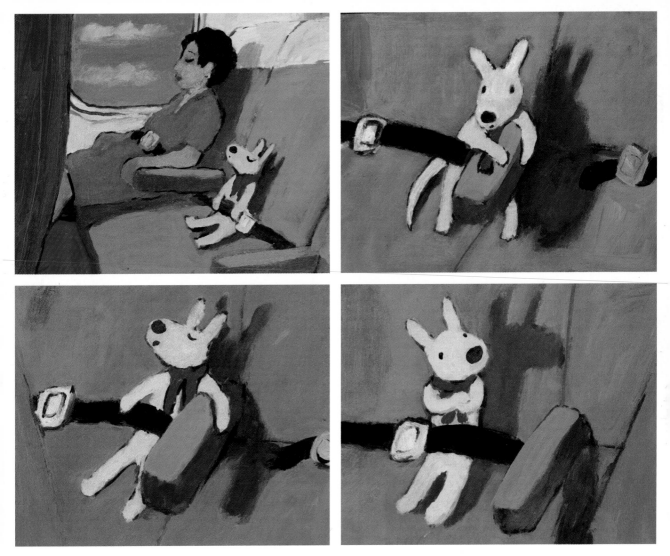

"But it's the plane that's moving, not me,"
I answered. After a while she moved to
another seat. I don't know why.

Then I had **three seats** all to myself! I could even lie down. So I took a little nap, but not for long.

Because a nice airplane lady came by with a big tray of food. Already it was time to eat!

I got lots of things.

A glass

A dish of beef, carrots, and peas.

A plastic knife, fork, and spoon

Salt

Cheese

Pepper

Water in a can

A roll

Butter

An empty mug

And a **giant** orange juice with a cherry

Cherry jam

A voice said, "Ladies and gentlemen...

...with the headphones in your
seat pocket, you may now
watch the movie
Cowboys Forever."
I put my headphones on, but I
had a little problem.

I couldn't see very much...

...until I found a way to
look over the big seat
in front of me.

It wasn't very comfortable, but the movie was so exciting, I didn't mind. Too bad I missed the end...

...I moved, and then so did my glass, and—"Oh no!" What a mess! The orange juice went everywhere.

The airplane lady came right away.
"It's okay," she said. "We'll fix this mess later.
What's your name?"
"Lisa," I answered, but I couldn't hear very well.
I even had orange juice in my ears.
Then she gave me a bath on the airplane.
What fun! She dried me off and said,
"Lisa, I have a surprise for you."

She took me into the cockpit
with the pilots. There were
little buttons everywhere,
even on the ceiling. I couldn't
touch them, but the pilot
told me what they do.
"You smell very nice," he said.
It was the soap.

When I went back to my seat,
I could see big buildings from my window.
But from this high, they looked like toys.
The pilot was right—the soap did smell good.

And so, all clean, I landed in America. I saw my uncle right away. He was holding a sign. We called my parents, but we forgot that it was the middle of the night in Paris. So we woke them up! "It's okay, Lisa," my dad said. "Have fun in New York!"